LITTLE
BEAUTY

First published 2008 by Walker Books Ltd
87 Vauxhall Walk, London SE11 5HJ

2 4 6 8 10 9 7 5 3 1

© 2008 Anthony Browne

The right of Anthony Browne to be identified as author/illustrator of this work has been
asserted by him in accordance with the Copyright, Designs and Patents Act 1988

This book has been typeset in Bookman

Printed in China

British Library Cataloguing in Publication Data: a catalogue record for this book
is available from the British Library

ISBN 978-1-4063-0866-2

LITTLE
BEAUTY

Anthony Browne

WALKER BOOKS
AND SUBSIDIARIES

LONDON • BOSTON • SYDNEY • AUCKLAND

Once upon a time there was a very special gorilla who had been taught to use a sign language. If there was anything he wanted he could ask his keepers for it by using his hands to sign. It seemed that he had everything he needed.

But he was sad.

One day he signed to his keepers

"I ...

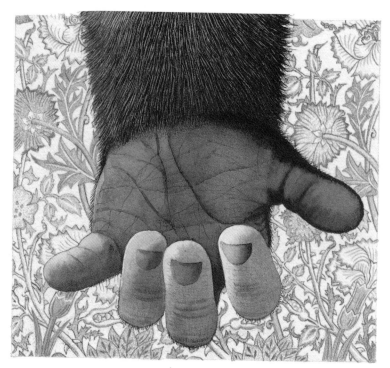

want ...

a friend."

There were no

other gorillas at

the zoo and at first the

keepers didn't know what to do.

Then one of them had

an idea.

They gave him a little friend

called Beauty.

"Don't eat her,"

said one of the keepers.

But
the
gorilla
loved
Beauty.

He gave her milk,

and honey.

And they were happy.

They did **everything** together.

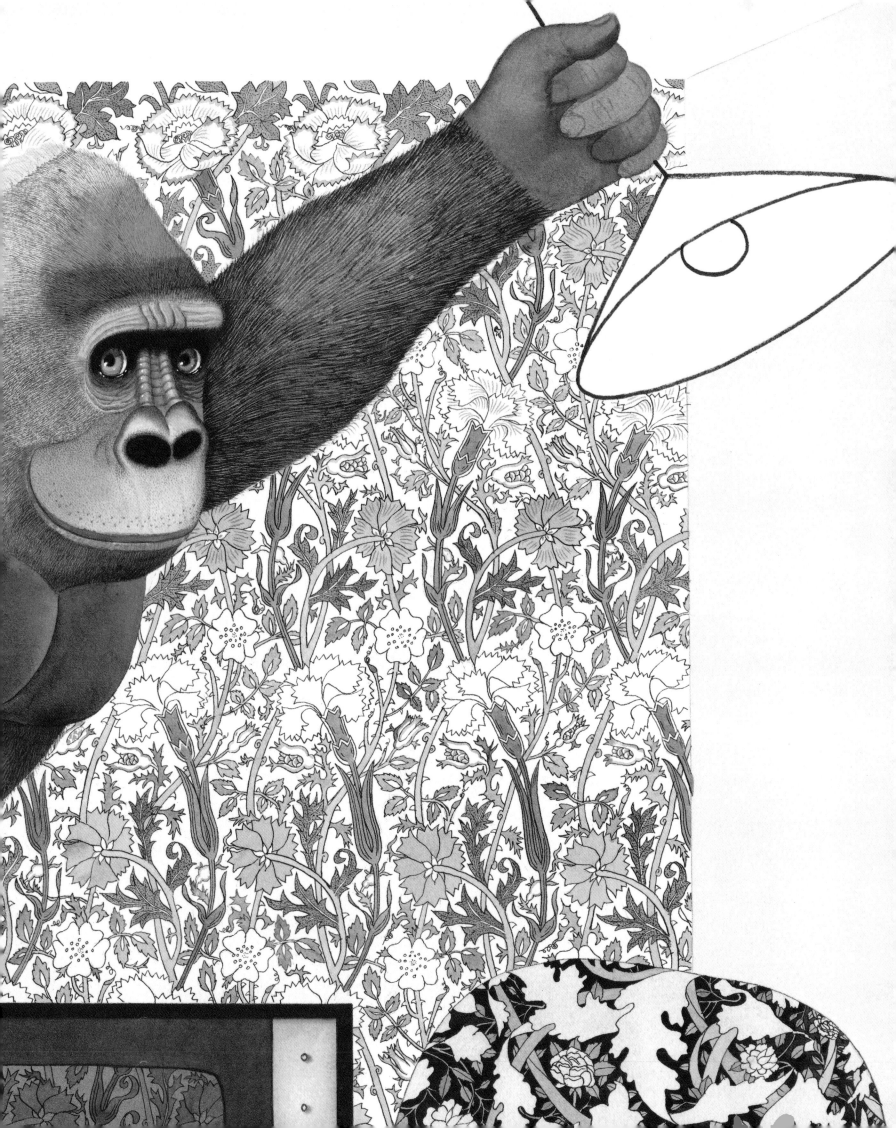

They were happy

for a long time ...

until one night they watched a film

together. The gorilla became

more and more upset,

and

then

very

ANGRY!

The keepers rushed in.

"Who broke the television?" said one.

"We'll have to take Beauty

away now," said another.

The gorilla looked at Beauty.

Beauty looked at the gorilla.

Then she started to sign...

"It …

was …

ME!

I broke

the television!"

Everyone laughed.

And do you know what happened?

Beauty and the gorilla lived

happily ever after.